To Elliott
from
Grandma
+
Granpa "99"

Copyright © 1996 by Michael Neugebauer Verlag AG, Gossau Zürich, Switzerland.
First published in Switzerland under the title *Teddybär*.
English translation copyright © 1996 by North-South Books Inc.
All rights reserved. No part of this book may be reproduced or utilized in any form or
by any means, electronic or mechanical, including photocopying, recording, or any
information storage and retrieval system, without permission in writing from the publisher.
First published in the United States, Canada, Great Britain, Australia, and New Zealand in
1996 by North-South Books, an imprint of Nord-Süd Verlag AG, Gossau Zürich, Switzerland.
Distributed in the United States by North-South Books Inc., New York.
Library of Congress Cataloging-in-Publication Data is available.
A CIP catalogue record for this book is available from The British Library.
ISBN 1-55858-662-8 (trade binding) 10 9 8 7 6 5 4 3 2 1
ISBN 1-55858-663-6 (library binding) 10 9 8 7 6 5 4 3 2 1
Printed in Germany

For more information about our books, and the authors and artists
who create them, visit our web site: http://www.northsouth.com

# Brigitte Weninger
# Ragged Bear
## Alan Marks

Translated by
Marianne Martens

A MICHAEL NEUGEBAUER BOOK
NORTH-SOUTH BOOKS / NEW YORK / LONDON

Once there was a
big honey-brown teddy bear.

He was old and worn, ragged
and torn, but his heart was
still full of love.

He spent most of his time sitting
in the corner, next to the old ball
and the wooden locomotive.

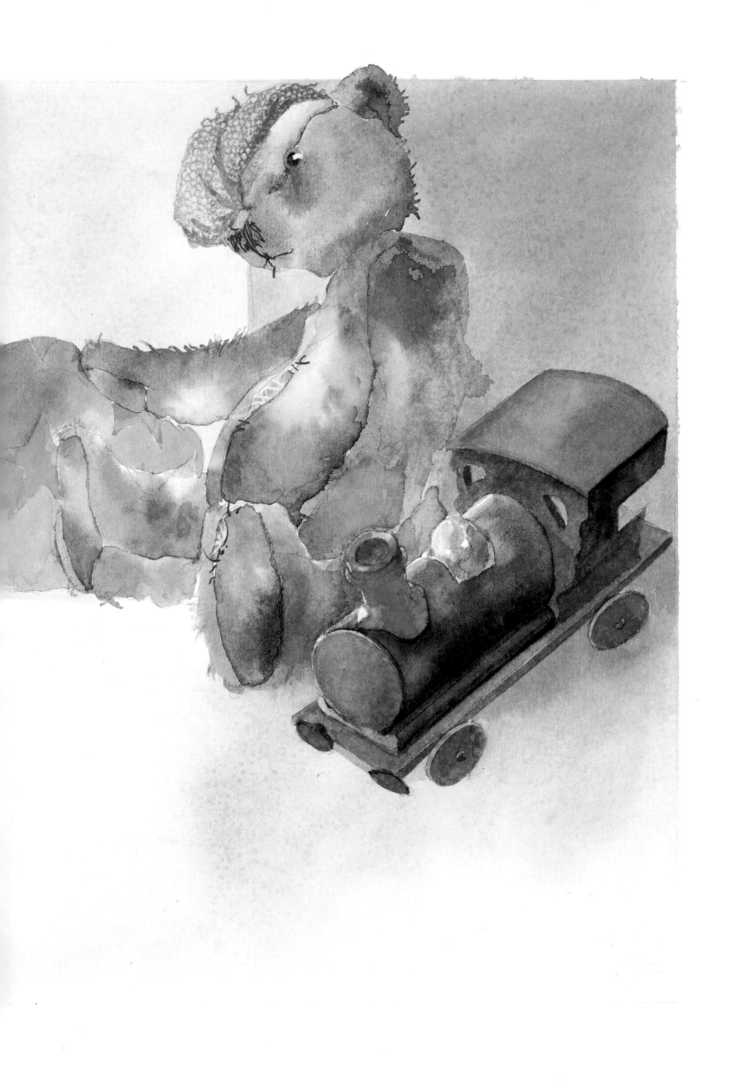

Once in a while the children
would play with him.

They would throw him high
in the air, until he landed
with a loud thump!

That was fun!

Sometimes they used him
as a pillow or as a doorstop.

Sometimes he was a tunnel
that the toy train drove under.

But when visitors came, the children would toss Teddy back in the corner.

They had much nicer toys to show their friends.

One day they brought Teddy
to the park. He rode in the tricycle
trailer with a puppet and a doll.

He was really happy.

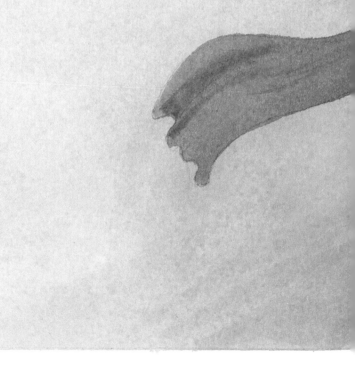

Then it started to rain,
and the children rushed
back home.

But they forgot Teddy!
He was left sitting on a park
bench all by himself.

Teddy cried, but because
he was already wet, no one
could see his tears.

He sat there for hours and
hours, soggy and miserable
and very, very sad, until
finally he fell asleep.

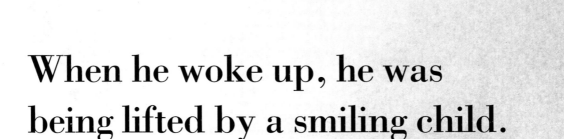

When he woke up, he was
being lifted by a smiling child.

Poor Teddy had looked so old
and ragged that someone had
thrown him away. But the
smiling child hugged him tight
and carried him to a new home.

There he was given a bubble bath, wrapped in a big towel, and set near the warm oven to dry.

Then he was lovingly brushed until his honey-brown coat shone like gold.

His nose was fixed, his ear
was repaired, and all the holes
in his stomach were sewn up.

And he was allowed to sleep in a bed!
He was hugged and cuddled, tucked
in tight, and kissed good night.

Later that night, as Teddy sat
in the glow of the moonlight, he was
the happiest teddy bear in the world.
He was still old—and a little bit
worn—but he was no longer ragged
and torn. And his heart was filled
with love.